Peppa Pig™

Around the World with Peppa

SCHOLASTIC INC.

Published by arrangement with Entertainment One and Ladybird Books, A Penguin Company. This book is based on the TV series *Peppa Pig*. *Peppa Pig* is created by Neville Astley and Mark Baker. Peppa Pig © Astley Baker Davies Ltd/Entertainment One UK Ltd 2003.

ISBN 978-1-338-13980-8

10 9 8 7 6 5 4 3 2 1

17 18 19 20 21

Printed in the U.S.A.
First printing 2017
www.peppapig.com

40

It is almost summer break.
Peppa is outside with her friends.

"What are you doing this summer?" asks Wendy Wolf.

"I am going to the park," says Peppa.

Peppa is excited. She is going to spend the summer jumping in lots of muddy puddles!

"I am going
to the jungle,"
says Pedro Pony.

"We are going to the desert,"
say Emily and Edmond Elephant.

"I am going to the mountains,"
says Danny Dog.

"I am going to the South Pole,"
says Suzy Sheep.

The next day, Peppa and her
family are driving to the park.

The car goes chugga-chugga-chugga . . .

Bang!

Clang!

Bonk!

"Oh, dear," says Daddy Pig.
"The car broke down."

Mummy Pig calls for help.
"Look!" says Peppa. "Here comes
Miss Rabbit!"

Miss Rabbit says it will take all day to fix the car.

"Do not worry," she says. "You can borrow my airplane!"

Everyone climbs into the airplane. Mummy Pig wants to drive.

"Are we supposed to be upside down?" asks Daddy Pig.

Neoooowww!

"Our next stop is the park,"
says Mummy Pig.
"To jump in muddy puddles!"
cheers Peppa.

Daddy Pig opens his map.
"I see some trees," he says.
"This must be the park."

"Where are the swings and slides?" asks Peppa.

"This looks like a jungle," says Mummy Pig.

Peppa's friend Pedro is in the jungle!

Mummy Pig lands the plane on the ground.

They find Pedro!
"The jungle is fun!" says Pedro.
"There are parrots and monkeys!"

"Can we visit my other friends, too?" asks Peppa.
"Of course!" says Mummy Pig.

Shooooom!

It is Daddy Pig's turn to fly the airplane. "Where next?" he asks.

"Danny Dog is in the mountains," says Peppa.

Danny Dog is climbing a big
mountain with Captain Dog.

Whhhiirrrrr!

Daddy Pig lands the airplane on the mountain.

"Hello, Danny!" shouts Peppa. "This mountain is very high!"

Peppa and her family fly away again. Soon, Daddy Pig sees spots of yellow sand.

"It must be the desert," he says.

Mummy Pig lands the airplane
on the sand. It is not easy!
They find Emily and Edmond
Elephant.

"We saw a lizard," says Edmond.
"It must be shy, because it ran
away."

Then, the lizard jumps on a
rock.

"There it is!" Daddy Pig shouts.
He scares the lizard away again.
   Doctor Elephant sighs. "Do you
have other people to visit?" he
asks.

Squeak!

Next, they fly to the South Pole.
　　There are lots of penguins. And Suzy is there!

Skkiiiiddd!
Screech!

"Peppa!" says Suzy.
Peppa and Suzy are best friends.
They are very happy to see each
other again.

Peppa has fun with Suzy and
the penguins. But Peppa still has
to go to the park.

Whooosh!

Peppa and her family get in the plane. They fly back around the world to get home.

"Hello, Miss Rabbit," says Peppa. "We flew all the way around the world!"

"Wonderful! Your car is working again," says Miss Rabbit.

Peppa and George climb inside.

Beep! Beep!

"Flying around the world was nice," says Peppa. "But something was missing . . ."

" . . . a muddy puddle!"